Sneaky Pie's Cookbook for Mystery Lovers

*Books by Rita Mae Brown
with Sneaky Pie Brown*

WISH YOU WERE HERE
REST IN PIECES
MURDER AT MONTICELLO
PAY DIRT
MURDER, SHE MEOWED
MURDER ON THE PROWL
CAT ON THE SCENT

Books by Rita Mae Brown

THE HAND THAT CRADLES THE ROCK
SONGS TO A HANDSOME WOMAN
THE PLAIN BROWN RAPPER
RUBYFRUIT JUNGLE
IN HER DAY
SIX OF ONE
SOUTHERN DISCOMFORT
SUDDEN DEATH
HIGH HEARTS
STARTING FROM SCRATCH:
A DIFFERENT KIND OF WRITERS' MANUAL
BINGO
VENUS ENVY
DOLLEY:
A NOVEL OF DOLLEY MADISON IN LOVE AND WAR
RIDING SHOTGUN
RITA WILL:
MEMOIR OF A LITERARY RABBLE-ROUSER

Sneaky Pie's Cookbook
for Mystery Lovers

—

Sneaky Pie Brown

Illustrations by Katie Cox Shively

BANTAM BOOKS
New York   Toronto   London   Sydney   Auckland

SNEAKY PIE'S COOKBOOK FOR MYSTERY LOVERS
A Bantam Book/May 1999

All rights reserved.
Copyright © 1999 by American Artists, Inc.

Book design by Glen M. Edelstein

Illustrations copyright © 1999 by Katie Cox Shively

No part of this book may be reproduced or transmitted in any form or by any means,
electronic or mechanical, including photocopying, recording, or by any information
storage and retrieval system, without permission in writing from the publisher. For
information address: Bantam Books.

Library of Congress Cataloging-in-Publication Data

Brown, Rita Mae.
Sneaky Pie's cookbook for mystery lovers / Sneaky Pie Brown.
p.   cm.
ISBN 0-553-10635-X
1. Cookery.   2. Cats—Anecdotes.   I. Title.
TX714.B79   1999
641.5—dc21   99-12337
                                                  CIP

Published simultaneously in the United States and Canada

Bantam Books are published by Bantam Books, a division of Random House, Inc. Its
trademark, consisting of the words "Bantam Books" and the portrayal of a rooster, is
Registered in U.S. Patent and Trademark Office and in other countries. Marca Registrada.
Bantam Books, 1540 Broadway, New York, New York 10036.

PRINTED IN THE UNITED STATES OF AMERICA

BVG   10 9 8 7 6 5 4 3 2 1

AUTHOR'S NOTE

CAT CUISINE IS very simple: meat, fish, and fowl. We are obligate carnivores, which means we must eat meat to stay healthy. Not that one has to eat as much as my sidekick Pewter, whose butt is so big you could show a movie on it. A kitty should know his or her limits.

I've included my favorite recipes plus a few for humans, dogs, and even a couple for horses.

Personally, I enjoy eating with humans but I refuse to eat with dogs. All that gobbling and swallowing chunks of food whole just turns my stomach. Then you spend the rest of the day listening to the symphony played by their intestines. Cats are ever so elegant compared to dogs.

I have personally tested each cat recipe, Tucker has tested the dog recipes and my veterinarian, Christopher Middleton, has checked them out, too. I've noted serving sizes only on those recipes for humans. The servings for cats, dogs, and a few others will vary from animal to animal. Tell your human to consider these treats. I'm assuming your regular diet has the protein and carbohydrates you need plus a touch of fat for the winter.

You'll find no recipes for mouse tartare, mole soufflé, or batwing soup. If I included them and your humans read this, the poor souls would faint dead away. You know how squeamish they are. Imagine telling them how to bite off a mouse's head? Get the smelling salts!

I hope you enjoy these and I wish you bon appétit and good health.

Yours in Catitude,
Sneaky Pie

RECIPES

Human

MRS. HOGENDOBBER'S ORANGE CINNAMON BUNS

Makes 24

1 ($^1/_4$–ounce) package active dry yeast
$^1/_4$ cup warm water
1 cup milk, scalded
$^1/_4$ cup granulated sugar
$^1/_4$ cup ($^1/_2$ stick) unsalted butter or margarine
1 teaspoon salt
$3^1/_2$ cups all–purpose flour
1 large egg
$^1/_4$ cup ($^1/_2$ stick) unsalted butter, melted
$^1/_2$ cup brown sugar
2 teaspoons cinnamon
$^1/_2$ cup raisins (optional)

TOPPING

$^2/_3$ cup brown sugar
$^1/_2$ cup (1 stick) unsalted butter or margarine
2 tablespoons light corn syrup
$^1/_3$ cup orange marmalade

1. Stir the yeast into the warm water and allow to soften (about 5 minutes).
2. Meanwhile, in a medium bowl, combine the milk, granulated sugar, $^1/_4$ cup butter, and salt. Set aside to cool.
3. Once the milk and sugar mixture has cooled, add $1^1/_2$ cups flour and beat well. Beat in the softened yeast and egg. Gradually stir in the remaining flour to form a soft, sticky dough.
4. Turn the dough out onto a lightly floured surface. Knead the dough briefly to form a smooth ball. Place the kneaded dough in a greased bowl, turning the dough several times to grease the surface. Cover the bowl with a damp cloth and let rise until doubled in volume, $1^1/_2$ to 2 hours.
5. While the dough is rising, combine all the ingredients for the topping in a small saucepan. Heat slowly over low heat, stirring often, until the brown sugar has dissolved. Pour the warm topping mixture into two 8 × 8 × 2-inch pans and set aside.
6. Turn the dough out onto a lightly floured surface and divide in half. Form half into a ball and let rest while rolling the other half into a 12 × 8-inch rectangle.
7. Brush the rolled dough with half the melted butter, sprinkle with $^1/_4$ cup brown sugar, 1 teaspoon cinnamon, and $^1/_4$ cup raisins, if using. Roll lengthwise into a tube and pinch the edges together to seal. Cut the roll crosswise into twelve 1-inch slices.
8. Roll the other ball into a 12 × 8-inch rectangle and repeat step 7.
9. Place the slices, cut sides down, on top of the topping

mixture in the prepared pans. Cover; let rise about 35 to 40 minutes. Preheat the oven to 350° F.

10. Remove the cover from the pans and bake the buns about 30 minutes, or until brown on top. Cool 2 to 3 minutes, invert on plates, and remove the pans.

WHAT A CHARACTER Mrs. Miranda Hogendobber is. She's a devout member of The Church of the Holy Light. She quotes scripture better than TV preachers. She sings in the choir. She fudges about her age but is finally brought up short by her fiftieth high school reunion. She helps out at the Crozet post office, where she is good friends with the much younger Mary Minor Harristeen, the postmistress. Widowed, Mrs. H. hasn't much money. She often brings in treats she's baked and Harry, as well as others, encourage her to sell her baked goods.

She finally does go next door to the convenience market and the proprietor says he'll give it a go. Well, her items are a hit, but none so much as these orange cinnamon buns. The success gives Mrs. H. what she calls "pin money."

I adore Mrs. H. because in my very first mystery, *Wish You Were Here,* she doesn't much care for cats and dogs. Mrs. Murphy, with help from Tucker, wins her over—but of course!

Cat

NEW YEAR'S TUNA

1 (6–ounce) can tuna packed in oil—unless you're
  fat, then use a can of tuna packed in water
¹/₂ pint half–and–half (Again, if you're a fat cat
  change that to an equal amount of 2% milk.)

1. Mix the ingredients together until mushy. Humans won't
   like it so you'll have it all to yourself. And although we
   all deserve a great big treat on New Year's Eve, this is
   probably enough for you and a feline friend.
2. Serve precisely at twelve o'clock midnight for a prosper-
   ous New Year.

As you know, I live in the South, which means that each New Year's Eve the humans are boiling black-eyed peas. The first food of the New Year they put in their mouths has to be black-eyed peas. You won't catch me eating a black-eyed pea or any other pea for that matter.

Most New Years around here are pretty much the same. Mother intends to stay awake until midnight. She places pots and pans by the door with a giant spoon, the idea being that after her mouthful of black-eyed peas, she goes outside and bangs the pots. The horses hate it, of course.

Out here in the country, people shoot rifles in the air, set off firecrackers, and make a great deal of noise. In the icy January air, with no leaves on the trees to muffle sound, those sounds carry. There's a lot of stall banging and loud complaints from the stable on New Year's Eve.

The New Year's Eve I remember best occurred when Pewter and I were kittens. The Corgi wasn't born yet. Mom waited until December 31 to buy a truck. Her first new truck. Pewter and I ran outside to admire the Ford F150 4 × 4. The metallic royal blue exterior seemed deeper against the white snow. The interior was a handsome beige. Naturally, our human was over the moon.

A mile and a half down our road lived a simpleminded neighbor two years older than God. I don't think I've ever seen a human that old before or since. No one called him by his last name because his uncle had been governor of Virginia back in the forties and a governor couldn't have a simpleminded nephew. As he was a short, energetic man, everyone just called him Banty.

Banty lived alone since his family had long been dead. He adored my mother because she spoke to him as though he was just like everyone else. Now, why he wanted to be just like anyone else mystifies me because the truth about Virginians is that one out of four is mentally ill. Think of your three best friends. If they're all right, then it's you! Mother's mother told her that and it's the God's honest truth—not that anyone from Virginia will admit it.

Anyway, Banty desperately wanted to be like everyone else. He'd visit and bring us fresh-grown catnip. What money his family had put aside for him had been exhausted decades ago—no one had ever expected him to live to such an advanced age. He cut his own wood for his wood-burning stove and his cookstove. He raised chickens and sold eggs. He also had goats for milk and he'd learned to make goat's milk soap, and a fine soap it was.

This particular New Year's Eve the evening temperature skidded into the teens. The day had been warmer, the low forties, and the snow melted a bit, which meant on top of the snow rested a treacherous layer of ice.

Mom had parked her new truck by the front door so she could look at it constantly. Before sunset she hopped into her old truck one last time, a worn 1972 Ford, and drove it down to the dealer. He would carry her home.

Banty, with a goat on a leash, a gift for Mom, walked up to the front door and knocked, but Mom wasn't home. We meowed. He opened the door a crack, thought better of it, and closed the door. The night was so bitter, he didn't want to leave the nanny goat tied to a fence. And if he turned the goat out in a pasture it would follow him home. So he opened the door of the brand-new truck and the goat jumped right in. Perfect. He slipped and slid down the driveway, walking the mile and a half back to his little house in the hollow.

Mom showed up in the driveway about an hour after that. She hopped out of the passenger seat and waved good-bye to the Ford dealer.

We watched from the picture window as she admired

her truck. She took a step closer. Stopped. Then moved as fast as we'd ever seen Mom move. Remarkable, really, given the ice. She opened the door to behold her present from Banty, and the fact that her truck now had no interior. The nanny goat even ate hunks out of the dash.

Mom lifted the goat out of the truck, sat down on the front steps, and cried. Finally she pulled herself together, walking the goat down to the garden shed. She couldn't put the nanny in with the horses because the scent of a goat will drive them crazy until they become accustomed to it. If you live in the city you might not know it but goats stink to high heaven.

She emptied out the garden shed, brought hay and straw up from the barn, falling down a couple of times in the process. It was getting colder and colder—so cold that the inside of your nose hurt when you breathed. Still, she was out there for over an hour.

When she reached the house her lips were blue. We loved on her and warmed her up as much as we could. She was distraught. How do you explain a situation like this to your insurance agent?

She called him at home. He said, "Happy New Year and don't worry."

Well, she felt somewhat better. She made Pewter and me some New Year's Tuna. Then she cooked herself black-eyed peas for luck. And you know, that turned out to be one of the best years we ever had, although I never have learned to tolerate the nanny goat, Princess Vandal.

Cat

SUNDAY SALMON DINNER

1 (7-ounce) can Norwegian salmon
1 (1.4-ounce) package dry cat food or $3/4$ cup if
   you don't use individual packages (use a fish
   flavor)
1 (8-ounce) package soft cream cheese

1. Chop the salmon into small pieces.
2. Mix in well with the dry cat food.
3. Cut the cream cheese into 4 squares and roll them into
   balls.
4. Roll the cream cheese balls in the mix until thoroughly
   covered. (Omit the cream cheese for a fat cat.)
5. Serve immediately or refrigerate in a tightly sealed container.

HUMANS ARE PACK animals. Cats are not. What makes living
with humans often difficult is they refuse to admit they are
pack animals—each human believes, deep down, that he or
she is a rugged individualist. This illusion is particularly ram-
pant in America.

I can prove this, should you doubt it, with a few exam-
ples:

Would any cat in her right mind wear stiletto heels?

Would any cat drink spirits until she or he puked?

Would any cat smoke cigarettes, thereby blunting her or his sense of smell? As for yellow teeth, I guess that wouldn't be so bad if you're a Burmese cat.

Would any cat crimp her hair until it looked as though she'd stuck her paw in a light socket?

Would any cat pay taxes even if the money showed up again in her or his community?

Would any cat give up meat?

Would any cat believe she or he is at the top of the food chain? This one just cracks me up.

Would any cat swear to be monogamous in front of a room full of other cats?

Would any cat have a facelift, tint whiskers, lengthen her or his tail?

Would any cat go down a hill on two sticks in the snow?

Would any cat go to war?

I rest my case.

Cat

JUST RIGHT CHICKEN

1 small whole chicken
2 tablespoons (1/4 stick) unsalted butter

1. Put the chicken in a large pot of cold water to draw the blood out. Depending on the size of the chicken, the time will vary, but leave the chicken in a covered pot for at least an hour. If you really want to be perfect, change the cold water every 15 minutes.
2. When the blood is out of the chicken, again fill the pot with 1 gallon of cold water, drop in the butter, and cook over medium to medium-high heat until the meat literally falls off the bones; about 3 hours. Set the chicken and stock aside to cool naturally.
3. Remove the chicken from the pot, cut into small pieces, and serve at room temperature. One small chicken will be enough for several meals.
4. Divide the stock in half. Refrigerate half and use later to lightly sprinkle over dry cat food—chicken flavor, of course.
5. Use the other half of the stock to make chicken soup for humans. Our favorite is Chicken Corn Soup (recipe follows).

Human

CHICKEN CORN SOUP
Serves 4 to 6

8 cups chicken stock
1 cup white rice
2 hard-boiled eggs, peeled and sliced
2 cups white corn (the kernels from about 3 ears)
3 tablespoons coarsely chopped fresh parsley
  (or 2 teaspoons dried)

1. In a large pot over high heat, bring the chicken stock to a boil. Stir in the rice, reduce the heat to medium-low, and simmer for 10 minutes.
2. Add the hard-boiled eggs, corn, and parsley. Reduce the heat to low, cover, and continue cooking until the rice is tender, 10 to 15 minutes longer.

CATS CAN EAT the soup, too, but humans like it best. Like all country recipes, you can fiddle with it to suit yourself, but it's real simple. Some people might prefer noodles to rice.

I like fish best of all but Pewter and Tucker like chicken. A Rhode Island Red led to Pewter's public disgrace.

Pewter visits the chicken coop daily, dreaming of

snatching a Silky or even one of the larger Rhode Island Reds. Knowing of Pewter's murderous intent, Mom covered the top of the chicken coop with small-gauge wire mesh. Keeps the hawks out, too. They'll swoop down and carry off a chicken so fast it will freeze your heart, especially if, like me, you're smaller than the hawk.

Last summer Mother hosted a picnic. Wooden trestle tables were set in parallel rows. Pretty red checkered tablecloths added to the color. Forty people came. The fun of the party was that each person had to bring a covered dish. Mom supplied the barbecue and the drinks. I don't know why parties are more fun when everyone pitches in, but they are.

The human ages ranged from two to ninety-one years old. The children played, watched the horses, and got into the chicken coop. Before I knew it, chickens were running everywhere, squawking, flapping their wings. All those insects flying in the air and crawling around on the ground were a picnic for them.

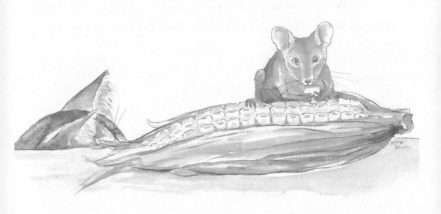

Mom knew there was no point in putting the chickens back until after the picnic because the children would let them out again by accident. So the chickens, under the guise of eating bugs, slowly began to work their way toward the picnic. They heard Mom's voice, which they associate with food. Personally, I think chickens are dumb as a post but Mom believes her chickens are intelligent. There's no point arguing.

Anyway, Pewter crouched low in the grass, cackling with delight. Why she thought her butt would be hidden from view by lying low is beyond me. That cat is fat. Of course, the chickens saw her and they recognized their tormentor. They paid her no mind.

One medium-sized red hen strayed away from the rest. As she pecked away, seizing white grubs and other delicacies, Pewter inched forward, then leapt up.

The hen cocked her head, fluffed her feathers, and emitted an earsplitting shriek. Scared Pewter. She landed in front of the chicken, who darted around behind her, grabbing her gray tail.

Now Pewter let out an earsplitting shriek. The huge Australorp rooster ran over and flapped his wings, kicking at Pewter with his spurs. Those things can cut you.

By now Pewter never wanted to see another chicken, but the red hen wouldn't let go. The humans were laughing so hard they were useless.

Finally, Mother pulled herself together and shooed the chicken from Pewter. The rooster flew up in her face, too. That offended Tucker, who growled, scaring the rooster, who flew onto one of the picnic tables, leaving a few well-aimed deposits.

The tip of Pewter's tail was blunted. Unfortunate, as her tail is short to begin with. (The artist for the Sneaky Pie mysteries, knowing of Pewter's vanity, makes her tail longer than it really is.)

Pewter vows to kill that hen, but she'll never do it.

The humans agreed it was the best picnic they'd ever attended.

*Cat**

SARDINE SANDWICH

1 slice of bread
1 tablespoon unsalted butter
1 (3.75-ounce) can sardines

1. Toast and butter the bread. Cut into eight equal-sized pieces.
2. Slice the sardines in half and place on the individual toast pieces.

MY DREAM IS to visit the fish market in Seattle someday. Mother swears it is the best fish market in America.

What would I do confronted with a fish five times bigger than I am (on ice, of course)? Drool. Of course.

*Some humans like sardines so you might have to share.

Dog

DOG BAIT

1 cup all-purpose flour
³/₄ cup cornmeal
1 garlic clove, finely chopped, or ¹/₂ teaspoon garlic salt
1 pound fresh liver

1. Preheat the oven to 350° F.
2. In a small bowl, mix together the flour, cornmeal, and garlic.
3. Cut the liver into small pieces, put in the blender, and puree. Combine with flour mixture.
4. Spread the mixture as evenly as possible in a greased baking pan or a 9-inch pie dish.
5. Bake for 30 minutes, or until done.
6. Remove and cut into pieces, sized to your dog's preference.

DOGS ARE MORE easily bribed than cats. At the Westminster Dog Show held at Madison Square Garden in New York City, Mom watched every possible bribe other than raw meat being offered. Barbara L. Powers, president of the Dachshund Club of America, was showing a stunning dog when she tossed a treat to Mom standing on the sidelines. Later, Mom asked her for the recipe, which I've recounted here, because the bait smelled good even to a human's nose.

I can testify that Barbara's bait works because Tucker will do anything Mother asks if there's a homemade liver treat for a reward. Imagine, selling your soul for liver.

Dog

BIG DOG'S DELIGHT

2 cups long-grain white rice
4 1/2 cups water
4 large garlic cloves, minced
1 large beef bouillon cube
1 cup venison, cut into 1/2-inch cubes and cooked

1. Put all the ingredients into a large pot and cook on high until the water boils.
2. Turn off at the boil, cover, and let steam for approximately 5 to 10 minutes. As soon as the top looks "dry," put the food into a storage container. If you overcook, it will be too dry, but you can always add more water in a pinch.
3. Serve 1 cup of the mixture in the morning and 1 cup at night either alone or mixed in with commercial dry food.

   Helpful Hints:
   •We put it in the microwave for 1 minute before serving.
   •You can substitute any kind of meat that you want. Living in the country, we luckily have a lot of deer

meat, which we freeze during deer season. It helps keep the food costs down.

APART FROM TUCKER, the Corgi, I also live with Tuxedo, a black and tan coonhound who, even I must admit, is a most remarkable dog. Then there's Godzilla, the two-year-old smooth-coated Jack Russell bitch, who is remarkable in entirely different ways.

Tuxedo and Godzilla haven't shown up in my mysteries yet for two reasons. One, Godzilla is conceited enough. Were she to get fan mail I don't think I could live with her. As it is Pewter receives almost as much fan mail as I do. And Tucker gets lots of photos from other Corgis.

Godzilla would be insufferable.

Tuxedo, on the other hand, may be the sweetest canine I have ever known. He's clean, intelligent, and biddable, just

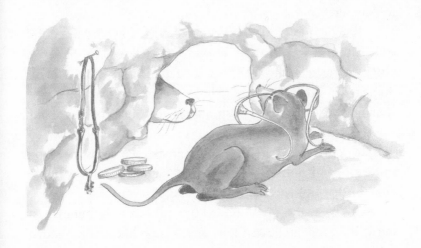

what a hound should be. And he's big! So if I put Tuxedo in a mystery, Tucker will get jealous. On the other hand, I can think of stories where a hound's special nose would solve the crime.

Once Mom lost her glasses. They cost $400 because they had a special light plastic lens, so she was upset. We searched the house high and low. I even crawled under the bureau in case they'd fallen behind. Not there.

We cleaned out the truck. Everything was pulled out, even the battery jumper cables. Nothing.

After a frenzied morning, we gave up.

Sitting on a fence post that afternoon, I saw Tuxedo loping across the pasture with something in his mouth. Godzilla, filthy, ran alongside.

They ran around the house. Mom was in the garden pulling weeds, the eternal chore. Tuxedo dropped the glasses next to her.

Happy, she gave everyone treats, and Big Dog's Delight for supper.

Tuxedo and Godzilla said the packrat down by the pond stole the glasses. Tuxedo tracked the glasses to her lair. Godzilla rushed into her den to get them out . . . a brave dog. She said that the stash included quarters, a bandanna, one spur with a leather spur strap, and a whole pile of the plastic rings you pull off to open a gallon of milk or distilled water.

It's curious what they find valuable. Possums carry off stuff, too, and Simon, in my mysteries, is based on a house possum that lived to the ripe old age of seven.

Crows steal shiny things all the time. I catch them pecking at the kiwi latches on the gates, a latch like a comma that

is supposed to be horseproof since there's a little ring that slips down to hold the lock. Two of the horses have figured out how to pick the kiwis but it's the crows that play with them. The silver shine attracts them.

During bird nesting season, Mom cuts four-inch squares of tinfoil and places them on fenceposts, the picnic table, and outdoor chairs. Then we hide and watch the crows swoop down to snatch them.

I confess to liking jewelry that's shiny. Gold is my favorite. I hide Mom's battered gold watch and necklace under the bed pillow. She always knows where to find them.

Cat/Dog

GOAT'S MILK FOR ORPHANED
KITTENS AND PUPPIES

I WAS TAKEN away from my cat mother too early and dumped at the SPCA, so my human mother had to feed me every four hours around the clock. She did this cheerfully for two weeks. After that she only had to feed me every four hours throughout the day.

You should always check with your veterinarian but here's what Mom mixed to keep me alive: powdered goat's milk mixed with enough water to make the consistency very smooth. Sounds easy but the powdered milk lumps up a little. Mom warmed it on the stove until it was tepid. Never, never make it really warm because what feels warm to a human finger feels a lot warmer to a baby's throat and stomach.

She bought a doll baby's bottle and nipped the end so the milk would flow. Then she put me on a towel on her lap so I could feed naturally, which is belly down. First she put a drop of milk on my nose, then she gave me the bottle.

When I grew a little bigger I could drink out of a shallow saucer.

Since my birth, Mom has nursed along two litters of hound puppies whose mothers died. All grew to be healthy seventy-pound hounds.

Occasionally, I still enjoy a taste of goat's milk, but it's rich and I can't drink much of it or I get a stomachache.

Human

MOM'S BIRTHDAY CAKE

Serves 8 to 10

This recipe is for people who love chocolate. Veterinarians say chocolate is bad for dogs. (Don't give me ideas.)

¹/₄ cup (¹/₂ stick) unsalted butter
¹/₄ cup Crisco
5 egg whites
1¹/₂ cups sugar
1 cup milk
3 cups all-purpose flour
3 teaspoons baking powder
1 teaspoon vanilla extract
1 recipe White Cream Icing (recipe follows)
1 recipe Unsweetened Chocolate Icing (recipe follows)
Toothpicks

1. Preheat the oven to 350° F.
2. In a small bowl, cream together the butter and Crisco and set aside.
3. In a medium bowl, beat the egg whites until stiff, then gradually add the sugar. Beat in the creamed butter and

Crisco. Gently stir in the milk, followed by the flour and baking powder, mixing until well blended and no lumps remain. Stir in the vanilla.

4. Pour into 2 greased and floured 9-inch round cake pans. Using a rubber spatula, spread the batter out evenly in each pan.

5. Bake on the third rack up from the bottom for 25 minutes, or until a cake tester comes out clean.

6. These layers will not be fluffy. This is a heavy, moist cake. When you bring them out of the oven, put a dish towel over them and cool to room temperature.

7. Once they're cool, turn the first layer onto a wire cake rack and cover the top and sides with $1/3$ of the White Cream Icing. Once it's set, pour $1/3$ of the Unsweetened Chocolate Icing on top of the already frosted layer. Let harden (in the refrigerator if necessary). To anchor the second layer, place toothpicks half in and half out of the first layer.

8. Carefully place the second layer on top of the first, pressing down until the toothpicks are completely hidden (they will keep it from sliding off). Spread the remaining White Cream Icing over the entire cake. Finally, cover with the remaining Unsweetened Chocolate Icing. Let harden (again in the refrigerator if necessary). Transfer the cake to a cake plate.

9. If the day is warm, put the cake in the coolest spot you have or the refrigerator, covered with a cake dish. It's important for the chocolate to harden.

10. When you serve the cake, whoever gets a toothpick gets a kitty kiss.

WHITE CREAM ICING

3/4 cup (1 1/2 sticks) butter, softened
2 cups confectioners' sugar, sifted
2 tablespoons milk or cream
1 teaspoon vanilla extract

1. In a mixer, cream the butter, then gradually add the confectioners' sugar until fully blended.
2. Stir in the milk or cream and vanilla until smooth and thick enough to spread on the cake.

UNSWEETNED CHOCOLATE ICING

4 ounces dark unsweetened chocolate

Melt the chocolate in a double boiler, being careful not to let it bubble. Spread (or drizzle) over the cake immediately.

I LOVE THIS cake. It's hard to make. Juts Brown, Mom's mother, made this every year on November 28, Rita Mae's birthday.

The trick is to put the cake in the refrigerator so the unsweetened chocolate will harden over the creamy vanilla icing. The combination of tastes is what makes the cake.

However, it's so slippery that after she spread the

unsweetened chocolate over the bottom layer, Juts put toothpicks in to hold the top layer in place. If she didn't, the top layer would look like the Leaning Tower of Pisa. Once, she spread the vanilla and unsweetened chocolate icings over the entire cake without anchoring it with toothpicks or even putting it in the icebox (Juts never called a refrigerator a refrigerator just like she never said zero; she said ought) and the top half slid off the bottom half, skidded across the table, and then slid onto the floor. Delicious. I'm still waiting for that to happen again.

Juts gave prizes to whoever got toothpicks in their cake slice. Usually the toothpicks were visible because Juts put in colored ones. It's odd what humans cherish; Mom still has some of her prizes: a little mechanical pencil, a rabbit's foot keychain, and a toy truck. Aren't people funny?

Dog/Human

DEVILED EGGS
Makes 1 dozen

6 hard—boiled eggs, peeled
1/4 cup mayonnaise
1 tablespoon yellow mustard
1 tablespoon cider vinegar
1 tablespoon sweet pickle relish (optional)
Salt and pepper
Paprika

1. Slice the hard-boiled eggs in half lengthwise.
2. Remove the yolks and place in a small bowl.
3. Add to the yolks the mayonnaise, mustard, vinegar, and pickle relish, if using. Stir until thoroughly mixed and fluffy-looking.
4. Season to taste with salt and pepper.
5. Pipe or spoon the mixture into the egg white halves.
6. Dust lightly with paprika.
7. Refrigerate and serve cold.

SOME CATS LIKE a raw egg mixed into their commercial food.

I am not one of them. Pewter craves eggs no matter how they are served.

Many dogs will eat an egg on the spot, smashing the shell.

I once saw Mom use an egg to train a horse. The mare, four years old, would "get light in the front" when she didn't do whatever you asked her to do. That means the front two legs come off the ground a bit. It's not the worst of sins but she'd discovered that this scared people.

Mother wanted her to walk over a log, that's all, walk over. Maybe the mare decided the log was going to bite her or maybe she was just plain lazy. I don't know. The first time she went up, Mom was ready with an egg in her hand. She rose up in her stirrups and smacked the egg right between the horse's ears. Well, that stunned the horse, who stood stone still. And from then on she would walk over that log when asked to.

This proves that horses are dumb.

Mother always takes up for the horses. She says they are grass eaters and their brains are organized differently than ours because humans and dogs and cats think like predators. I still think they're slow in the head.

Cat/Dog/Human

Serves 4

MOTHER'S FRIED CHICKEN

1 package chicken pieces or 1 broiler chicken, cut into
serving pieces (legs, wings, thighs, breasts)
2 cups chicken breader mix
1/4 cup Old Bay seasoning
Salt and pepper
Vegetable or peanut oil

1. Thoroughly rinse the chicken pieces and pat them dry.
2. Mix the chicken breader mix and Old Bay seasoning in a large brown paper bag.
3. Add salt and pepper to taste.
4. Heat the oil in a large chicken fryer or deep fryer until hot but not smoking.
5. Dredge the chicken pieces in the breader mix and add to the hot oil. Fry until golden brown.
6. Drain on paper towels.
7. Put on a baking sheet and bake at 350° F. for 20 to 30 minutes, or until cooked through.

THIS SATISFIES YOUR need for crunchy sounds . . . and your need for meat. Humans will eat it, too. Caution: Cats and dogs should not eat bones. Those tiny chicken bones can splinter in your intestine and kill you. Ask your human to cut the chicken off the bone.

Mother says there are two ways to make a man fall in love with you. One is to serve him good fried chicken. The other is to wear red and yellow. There's a folk saying, "Red and yellow, catch a fellow." I don't know where it came from or why those colors but Mom absolutely believes it.

She also wishes on stars and carries a lucky rabbit's foot. Wasn't lucky for the rabbit, I can tell you.

Humans aren't rational but since they only talk to one another, they don't know it.

Some other cherished beliefs of my human:

An itchy palm means money's coming your way.

If your nose itches, someone is talking about you.

A blackbird pecking on a windowpane means someone in the family will die soon.

Cocktail parties are an excellent way to weaken men.

If a shadow crosses your mirror a secret will be revealed.

If any animal brings you a human hand, you will come to great power.

When visiting a human in his or her new home, bring an offering of salt in one container and sugar in another. (Mom always brings a loaf of fresh bread, too.)

Never give anyone an empty purse. Always put a dollar in it.

On Christmas Eve at midnight, go to the stable and speak to the horses and cattle. They will speak back because animals first recognized Jesus. Took the Wise Men until January 6th.

I could fill a book with these superstitions. There's no point arguing with a human over something like this. You have to humor them.

Rabbit/Human

RABBIT FOOD
Makes 1 large salad

1 head Boston lettuce
1 head arugula
¹/₄ cup mustard greens
¹/₂ cup toasted sunflower seeds
¹/₂ cup cubed mild Cheddar cheese
¹/₂ cup chopped fried bacon, drained
Pinch of capers
Simple Dressing (recipe follows)

1. Chill the salad bowl while you wash and dry the lettuce and greens.
2. Tear the lettuce and greens into bite-size pieces.
3. Add the other ingredients and toss gently.
4. Serve with Simple Dressing.

SIMPLE DRESSING

Extra—virgin olive oil
High—quality vinegar (Mom especially likes raspberry
  vinegar)

Mix three parts oil to one part vinegar to taste. Flavored
  oils, such as lemon or garlic, can add a nice twist to the
  dressing. If you're feeling adventurous, try adding a dash
  of orange juice, a tablespoon of mustard, a teaspoon of
  shaved fresh ginger, or even a little white wine.

OCCASIONALLY ONE MUST serve food to a herbivore. They're
so weird. Nothing could induce me to eat this salad, although
Pewter will pick out the bacon and cheese. Humans like it
fine, as do rabbits. I knew a turtle once who ate a salad but
he also ate a chicken's foot. It's probably not a good idea to
dwell on his gastronomic feats.

Dog/Human

NELSON COUNTY APPLE CRISP
Serves 6

5 to 6 juicy apples (about 2½ pounds), peeled,
  cored, and cut into eighths
2 teaspoons lemon juice
½ cup (1 stick) unsalted butter, cut into very small
  pieces
¾ cup pastry flour
1 cup sugar
1 teaspoon cinnamon
¼ teaspoon grated nutmeg
Whipped cream or Nutmeg Sauce (recipe follows)

1. Preheat the oven to 375° F.
2. In a medium bowl, toss the apples with the lemon juice.
3. Arrange the apples in a greased pie plate or shallow baking dish (8 × 8 × 2 inches).
4. In a medium bowl, blend together with your fingers the

butter, flour, sugar, and spices as for a piecrust. Press this mixture over the top of the apples.

5. Bake until golden brown and the juices are bubbling, 1 to 1¼ hours.

6. Serve with whipped cream or Nutmeg Sauce.

NUTMEG SAUCE

1 tablespoon unsalted butter
1 cup sugar
1 tablespoon all—purpose flour
1 teaspoon grated nutmeg
Pinch of salt
2 to 3 tablespoons water

1. In a small saucepan, over medium heat, melt the butter. Whisk in the sugar, flour, nutmeg, and salt. Gradually whisk in the water, whisking until well combined.
2. Allow the mixture to cook at a rolling boil for 5 minutes, stirring frequently.
3. Remove from the stove and serve while hot over the apple crisp.

I DON'T KNOW why the dogs like this but they do.

Horses love apples. However, never turn a horse out in a field with an apple tree that's still producing fruit because the horses will eat apples that aren't ripe, tearing them off the branches, or they'll eat the overripe fruit that's fallen to the ground. Either way, you've got a sick horse.

I enjoy sitting in an apple tree in springtime. The activity dazzles me—bees everywhere, caterpillars, and birds chasing after the caterpillars. For a cat, an apple tree is a little bit of heaven.

Human

BUCKINGHAM MAYONNAISE
(Recipe from 1872)

Makes $1^2/3$ cups

$^1/2$ cup distilled white vinegar
2 tablespoons ($^1/4$ stick) unsalted butter
1 large egg
1 cup vegetable oil
2 tablespoons dry mustard
1 tablespoon all-purpose flour
Pinch of salt

1. In a medium saucepan over medium heat, heat the vinegar and butter together until boiling.
2. Meanwhile, in a medium bowl, whisk together the egg, sugar, and dry mustard. Whisk in the flour and salt.
3. Whisk the egg mixture into the boiling vinegar mixture. Boil until thick, whisking constantly, about 2 minutes.

MOTHER LIKES TO eat mayonnaise bread. She piles the mayo on the bread, happy as she can be. I, too, love mayonnaise and if I don't get a teaspoonful, I steal her mayonnaise bread when she's not looking. If you're in danger of getting caught, throw the bread on the floor and blame the dogs.

Cat/Dog/ Human

CHRISTMAS GOOSE

Serves 6

1 (8–pound) freshly dressed goose, washed, patted dry, extra fat, neck, gizzard removed (Cut off long neck skin.)

Salt and pepper

Potato and Bread Stuffing (recipe follows) or use a packaged mix

4 cups water

2 tablespoons cornstarch dissolved in ¹/₄ cup water

1. Preheat the oven to 350° F.
2. Sprinkle the salt and pepper inside the cavity of the goose. Fill the cavity with the prepared stuffing. Secure the stuffed cavity with skewers.
3. Place the bird, breast side down, on a wire rack in a roasting pan. Add 2 cups water to the pan and cover with heavy-duty foil.
4. Roast for 4 hours.
5. During the last 20 minutes of baking time, increase the

temperature to 450° F.; remove the foil and turn breast side up to brown.

6. Remove the goose from the roasting pan and place on a serving platter while making the gravy. Make the gravy by removing the fat from the roasting pan. Place the roasting pan over the burners on top of the stove and add 2 cups water to the brownings. Thicken with the cornstarch dissolved in water. Stir over low heat until all the brownings have dissolved and the mixture has thickened.

POTATO AND BREAD STUFFING

Makes 6 cups of stuffing

$^1/_2$ cup water
$^1/_2$ cup chopped celery with leaves
$^1/_4$ cup chopped onion
1 teaspoon salt
$^1/_4$ teaspoon freshly ground black pepper
1 tablespoon chopped parsley
Pinch of saffron
2 cups mashed potatoes
3 eggs, lightly beaten
2 cups fresh bread cubes

1. In a 1-quart saucepan, bring the water to a boil; add the celery, onion, salt, pepper, parsley, and saffron. Boil approximately 7 minutes, until the celery is clear.

2. In a large bowl, lightly mix the celery mixture with the potatoes, beaten eggs, and bread cubes until well combined.

3. At this point, the mixture is ready to be stuffed into the cavity of the bird. If used as a side dish, bake in a buttered dish in a preheated oven at 350° F. for 30 minutes.

THIS RECIPE HAS been in the Buckingham family (Mother's maternal family) since their beginnings in America, 1620. Written first in the family Bible, it was updated when non-wood-burning stoves became popular. As the first Buckingham (Thomas) fled England, we figure it's an old English recipe. The English consider goose a great delicacy.

You've got to love a people who, at the end of the fourteenth century, made Dick Whittington the Lord High Mayor of London because he had a smart cat.

Because it's special and takes time, we only cook a goose for Christmas, which brings up another Buckingham peculiarity. They always have at least one tabby cat. They believe that a tabby cat helped the Blessed Virgin Mother at Christmas. When baby Jesus couldn't get to sleep the tabby hopped in the manger and purred the baby to sleep while helping keep him warm. The cat's reward was to have an M marked on her forehead, Mary's cat. To this day some tabby cats have the M. They are descendants of Mary's cat. I have the M on my forehead.

Human

JUTS'S MORTGAGE
MINCEMEAT
Makes enough filling for 2 pies

1 pound chuck meat, cut into small cubes
1 cup cider
1²/₃ cups New Orleans—style molasses
8 apples, cored, peeled, and cut into small cubes
6 ounces beef suet
2 cups currants
3 cups seedless raisins
1 cup citron, diced fine
2¹/₂ cups sugar
1 cup sipping whiskey
¹/₂ teaspoon ground cloves
3 teaspoons cinnamon
¹/₂ teaspoon ground mace
¹/₄ teaspoon freshly ground black pepper
1 tablespoon salt
¹/₂ tablespoon freshly grated nutmeg
Zest from 1¹/₂ lemons

1. In a large Dutch oven, bring the meat and cider to a boil over medium-high heat. Skim off the froth and stir in the molasses. Stir in everything else, reduce the heat to low, and stir, and stir, and stir every 15 minutes for 3 to 5 hours, or until the mixture is very thick and jamlike.
2. Naturally you can pour in more liquor to suit your taste. Keep tasting, as this is a seat-of-your-pants recipe. When it suits you, it's done.
3. Turn off the heat and let it cool down.

YOU CAN PUT it in a piecrust or serve it just like it is. It gets better with time, but do refrigerate it and warm it up when you next serve it, although you can eat it cold. This is Tucker's favorite recipe.

Mother tells this tale of Juts's mincemeat (Juts Brown was my mother's mother). It was the Depression and everything was going to hell in a handbasket. Juts desperately needed a mortgage. She invited the banker to the house for Christmas Eve—the Browns always threw open their doors on Christmas Eve, which meant the folks in town were mixed up worse than a dog's breakfast and loved every minute of it.

Her eggnog was as famous as her mincemeat. For every egg she added a glass of brandy and a glass of whiskey.

By the time the banker ate her mincemeat and knocked back a couple of glasses of eggnog, Juts had her mortgage.

Dog

DOG COOKIES

3 cups whole wheat flour
1 cup wheat germ
1 cup bran flakes
1 cup soy flour
1 cup cornmeal
1 cup grits
1 tablespoon active dry yeast
1 cup sunflower seeds, ground
1 egg or equivalent egg substitute
1 $^3/_4$ cups broth or water
$^1/_4$ cup canola oil
1 cup nonfat dry milk

1. Combine all the ingredients in a large mixing bowl.
2. Roll or pat out to $^1/_4$- to $^1/_2$-inch thickness. Cut with a
   dog bone–shaped cookie cutter or into 1 × 3-inch strips.
   Place on a well-oiled baking sheet.
3. Bake at 300° F. for 45 minutes.
4. Turn off the heat and leave in the hot oven for 30 minutes or more to dry.

A DOG'S NUTRITIONAL requirements are very different than a cat's. For one thing, a dog will eat almost anything. If it doesn't sit well, they just throw it up and look for more food. I think this is absolutely gross.

They love dried smoked pigs' ears. You couldn't pay me to eat one of those things. Nor will I eat carrion. This alone proves the superiority of cats—although, I confess, I love Tucker, the Corgi, despite her food habits. We were babies together. People who say cats and dogs don't get along don't know what they're talking about. If we're raised together, we do.

Dog

THE DOG'S DINNER

Take the leftovers from these recipes, toss all of them in a dish, and feed. (Hee hee.)

Cat/Human

SALMON PIE
Makes 1 pie

1 (8–inch) piecrust
2 tablespoons (¹/₄ stick) unsalted butter or margarine
2 tablespoons all–purpose flour
2 cups 2% milk
1 (7–ounce) can salmon
¹/₂ (6–ounce) package frozen peas
2 cups potato chips

1. Bake the piecrust at 425° F. until lightly browned. Take out of the oven and reduce the heat to 375° F.
2. In a saucepan, melt the butter over low heat. Stir in the flour until there are no lumps and add the milk. Stir until thickened.
3. Drain the salmon and mix with the sauce.
4. Stir in the frozen peas and pour the mixture into the prepared piecrust.
5. Lightly crush the potato chips and spread evenly over the salmon mixture.
6. Bake for about 20 minutes, or until bubbly.

IF YOU DON'T want to bake a pie, you can leave out the peas and potato chips, roll into small balls, and eat immediately. Humans won't eat it that way.

If you don't like salmon, and some cats don't, you can substitute lamb, beef, or tuna. Personally, I don't like beef except for organ meats, but other cats crave beef. There's no accounting for taste.

Cat

VEAL KIDNEY

1 fresh kidney, washed and diced

1. If your human won't dice the raw kidney, have him or her put the kidney in a pot, cover with water, and boil. After 15 minutes, turn off the heat and let cool.
2. Remove the meat and cut into small pieces.
3. You can pour this over your crunchies cold or warm it up.

I ENJOY KIDNEY any time of year but Mother won't make it in the summer. The aroma overpowers her.

As you've noticed, humans have a peculiar sense of smell. Their olfactory sense is underdeveloped. To further impair their noses, they smoke and wear perfume or cologne. But the scent of kidney in summer is too much for Mom, who has a good nose for a human.

I was reading *The Intelligence of Dogs* the other day, and I quote, "The scenting ability of hounds is truly remarkable. The average dog has around two hundred twenty million scent receptors in its nose, as compared to only five million for humans." And just think, a hound has a better nose than other dogs.

On the issue of scent, I concede that dogs are far superior to cats.

Horse

MOLASSES MASH

$^1/_4$ cup dry molasses
$^3/_4$ bucket beet pulp
Warm water

1. Mix the dry molasses through the beet pulp, then add warm water almost to the top of the pail. Allow to sit overnight.
2. When you come into the barn in the morning, reach down in the pail with your hands and turn the mixture over again.
3. For a 16-hand horse, add $^1/_2$ cup of the molasses mash to his or her regular feed.

SOME PEOPLE FEED their horses beet pulp daily and no sweet feed. We use it as a treat since most horses enjoy the molasses taste.

Mom's grandfather used to make a bran mash: $^3/_4$ bucket high-quality bran, $^1/_2$ cup dry molasses, warm water, and 1 ounce brandy.

If a horse is stall bound, the last thing you want to do is

fill them up on bran. He used the mash as a reward, feeding it once a week out in the pasture.

Horses' digestive systems are very different from cats'. The best thing in the world to feed a horse and keep it from colic is good-quality hay and lots of water. If you live in an area where the grass has plenty of nutrients, like Kentucky, with all that limestone in the soil, that's the best of the best. Of course, turn a horse out on new spring grass and they'll eat themselves sick. Remember what I said about horses being stupid . . .

Horses are grazers. Their ideal situation is to eat and walk, eat and walk. My ideal situation is to eat in one spot.

Pewter likes to sit on the fence post and call the horses to her. One day she was sunning herself on the fence, eyes closed, dozing, when one of the babies, Sidekick, snuck up. He tiptoed almost like a cat, got right behind her, then blew air out of his nostrils. Pewter shot three feet straight up in the air. Scared the horse as much as he'd scared her.

She raced to the house and he ran down and jumped into the pond.

He's not a baby now, he's 16.3 hands, half Thoroughbred and half Dutch Warmblood. His sense of humor has grown with his size. He likes to steal hats off humans' heads. He pulls bridles off bridle hooks, carries them to the other end of the stable, drops them, and returns for another one. He knows how to open doors, too. Last summer he jumped out of his three-board fence pasture—he can "jump the moon" effortlessly— walked up to the back of the house, stepped over the stone wall, continued across the patio, and opened the back door. The wood floor baffled him, though. He'd start to come into the kitchen, then back off.

Tucker ran for Mother, who almost fainted when she saw Sidekick. She had visions of those steel shoes on her maple floors. She didn't yell at him but he knew he'd been a bad boy so he turned around, stepped back over the stone wall, trotted across the lawn, and flew over the stone jump at the end of the lawn. He hung out at the old Indian spring all day, hoping we'd forget his misdeed.

I love horses because they have such a wonderful sense of humor.

Cat/Human

SNEAKY'S FAVORITE OYSTER'S

1 quart fresh oysters
1/2 cup coarse cornmeal
4 bay leaves
Pinch of salt and pepper
1 egg, beaten
3 tablespoons Crisco (you may need more, so keep
some handy)

1. Thoroughly wash the oysters.
2. Crumble the 4 bay leaves into the cornmeal, and toss in the salt and pepper.
3. Mix in the egg.
4. Spread the moistened meal on a piece of wax paper or foil.
5. Dredge the oysters with the batter until completely covered.
6. Put the Crisco in a number 5 frying pan (or whatever you like) and melt over high heat. When the Crisco is hot, turn the heat down to medium-high and add the oysters, turning them once. Depending on how hot the

fat is (every stove is a little different), they should be done in 10 minutes.

HUMANS MIGHT LIKE more spices, but then I won't eat the oysters. This way we can both eat them.

I like shellfish and am happy with any popped right out of the shell. Oddly enough, Pewter won't eat them. She eats everything else, including broccoli.

I also happen to know that she knocked over the aquarium and ate the fish. She denies it, but who else would have done it? Mother was so distressed she has never bought another aquarium.

I weakened when I saw those fish flopping around on the floor. Seemed silly to let them go to waste but I didn't break the aquarium. I swear it. It really was Pewter.

Cat

PEWTER'S FAVORITE CRAB

1 average—size box of white rice
1 pint fresh crabmeat or crab substitute

1. Cook the rice according to package directions. As it cools, cut the crabmeat into small bites.
2. Mix together.

IF WE GIVE Pewter the whole amount, she'll eat it. Instead, we give her a big helping and put the rest in the refrigerator.

Pewter also came from the SPCA. She was a tiny, round gray ball with cigarette burns on her body. Mother brought her home, to my disgust, but when Pewter told me her tale of abuse I decided another cat wouldn't be that bad.

She loves Mother, sits in her lap, follows her around, and is the jolliest cat I have ever known.

Some stories do have happy endings.

Horse

HORSE COOKIES

1 cup sweet feed
2 to 3 cups wheat bran
Dash of salt
1 cup dark molasses
4 carrots, grated
1/2 cup brown sugar
1 cup applesauce
Big dash of cinnamon

1. In a big bowl, mix the sweet feed with 2 cups of bran and a dash of salt.
2. In a separate bowl, mix the molasses, carrots, brown sugar, applesauce, and cinnamon.
3. Slowly pour the wet mixture into the dry mixture, stirring to form a thick dough. The batter is supposed to be a bit loose, but if it's really wet, add up to another cup of bran.
4. Lightly grease a cookie sheet.
5. Shape batter into portions the size of a half dollar, squeezing out excess liquid if needed.
6. Bake at 300° F. for 1 hour.

7. Flip the cookies over and bake 45 minutes more, until dry and golden brown.
8. Check on them frequently to avoid overbaking. Horses don't appreciate burnt cookies!

THERE ARE MANY variations of this horse cookie recipe and all are good.

Most horse recipes involve molasses. Recently people have begun collecting these, handed down verbally from generation to generation. Most are similar, since a horse's stomach doesn't need variety. Consistency is far more important.

Humans, on the other hand, like variety.

If you change your horse's diet, you should do it very slowly. For instance, if you've been feeding only beet pulp and want to switch over to sweet feed, mix a small portion of sweet feed in the pulp.

It's wise to do this changeover, adding a bit more sweet feed, over a two- to three-week period.

An abrupt change in diet can make horses sick, which, for them, can be fatal. I can throw up a bad mouse. A horse can't throw up, hence colic and other intestinal problems, which are quite terrible for them.

They can't eat any meat. Period.

Their teeth are for grinding, so the dentist must come and file off the rough edges once a year at a minimum.

I get my teeth cleaned about once every five years. It's easier being a cat.

As cats love horses so horses love cats because we are quiet and respectful. Dogs rush around barking or nipping (very naughty) but we tiptoe into stalls or sit on a tack trunk and chat with our equine friends.

I especially enjoy talking with the horses because they see so much more than I do. Their eyes are big and they can see behind, too, whereas I focus intently on what's in front of me. That's the difference between predator and prey animals.

Humans spend too much time talking about the food chain. Once we are full we can all get along just fine. They would do well to learn that.

Here's to full bellies, endless frolic, and laughter for all animals.

Katie Shively

ABOUT THE AUTHOR

SNEAKY PIE BROWN resides on a farm in Afton, Virginia. She is at work on her next Mrs. Murphy mystery when she isn't lording it over the other farm animals.